Nigel *and* *the* Moon

Nigel *and*

the Moon

By Antwan Eady

Illustrations by Gracey Zhang

KT KATHERINE TEGEN BOOKS
An Imprint of HarperCollins Publishers

For my mom and dad, Viola and Peter. For my siblings and their young dreamers.
And for you, dear reader. One day you will unlock the secret desires
of your heart and fervently pursue them. —A.E.

To all yet to be realized dreams: the moon is always listening. —G.Z.

Katherine Tegen Books is an imprint of HarperCollins Publishers.

Nigel and the Moon
Text copyright © 2022 by Antwan Eady
Illustrations copyright © 2022 by Gracey Zhang
All rights reserved. Printed in the United States of America.
No part of this book may be used or reproduced in any manner whatsoever without written permission except
in the case of brief quotations embodied in critical articles and reviews. For information address HarperCollins
Children's Books, a division of HarperCollins Publishers, 195 Broadway, New York, NY 10007.
www.harpercollinschildrens.com

Library of Congress Control Number: 2021933138
ISBN 978-0-06-305628-2

The artist used ink, gouache, and watercolor paint to create the illustrations for this book.
Typography by Chelsea C. Donaldson
21 22 23 24 25 PC 10 9 8 7 6 5 4 3 2 1
❖
First Edition

At night, he tells the moon his dreams.
And here his dreams are safe.

And I'm an astronaut.

"Hi. My name's Nigel.

A dancer.

A superhero too."

Among the stars, he twirls, quietly soaring
in the still of the night.
With pride, his chest swells.
And his eyes, they glow. His smile, it shines.

Now the moon isn't the brightest
body in the sky.
Nigel is. And so are his dreams.

But even with dreams so bright,
he isn't ready for the world to see.

The first day of career week has arrived.
And Nigel's school takes a trip to the library.

Book after book, page after page, his classmates choose their favorite jobs.

Nigel flips . . . and he flips . . . and he flips again, but a dancer like him cannot be found.

On the second day, his class shadows their parents at work.
House after house, block after block, Nigel follows his mom.

With feet planted on the ground, Nigel looks to the sky.
And the distance from here to there grows larger still.

Back in his bed, he searches for the moon.
In the dark hue of the night, he finds it
once more.
And there, between the moon and him,
his dreams are waiting.

"Tomorrow, I'll tell the world," he says.
Yet he quivers at the thought.

On the third day, the teacher asks, "What would you like to be when you grow up?"

"A doctor!"

"An engineer like my dad!"

"A veterinarian!"

Nigel shrinks in his chair. "I—I don't know."
He can't bring himself to whisper the word: *superhero*.

But later that night, he tells the moon his hopes.
And out the window they glide, far, far away
where no one can pull them down.

"One day, I'll land on the moon."

"Dance ballet."

"And wear my cape with honor."

But Nigel also worries, and he shares that with the moon.
"What if I wish to be too many things?" he wonders.

When the sun rises, he packs his
dreams away again.

On the fourth day, his teacher asks,
"What are your parents' careers?"

"My mom's a surgeon."

"My dad's a weatherman."

"My mother's the president
of a big candy company."

Now all eyes are on Nigel.

"My parents—"

He pauses. Then asks to be excused.

That night, he tells the moon his truth.

"I'm scared."

"My parents don't have fancy jobs."

"Will my class laugh if I tell them?"

The next morning, Nigel slowly makes
his way down the stairs.

It's easy to tell the moon his truth.
It's easy to tell the moon his dreams.
But Nigel's not ready to tell the world.

"Dream big, Son," Dad says.

"And be proud of who you are," says Mom.

The final day of career week is here.
And some special guests have arrived.
An author.
A chef.
And an architect too.

"But that's not all," the teacher says. "Come in, Mr. and Mrs. Strong."

Nigel slides down in his chair, but a shy smile grows across his face.

His mom introduces herself first.

"I'm a postal carrier, and I help connect people around the world. Love letters, birthday cards, postcards, and more—*I* deliver them all."

His dad follows.

"I'm a truck driver. Most days, it feels like I'm driving a monster truck. *Vroom!*"

The class erupts in laughter.

Looking around the room, Nigel can tell it's the good kind.

"Above all," his dad adds, pointing at his son.
"Raising Nigel's been the best job we've ever had."
With pride, Nigel's chest swells.
His eyes, they glow. His smile, it shines.

At night, he tells the moon his dreams.
But today—

He takes a stand. "I'd like to say something."
Nigel joins his parents in front of the class.

"I want to be an astronaut on the moon or a dancer on the stage. And when the world needs a superhero, *I* can be that too."

At night, he tells the moon his dreams.
But telling the world isn't so scary after all.